THE NATIONAL POETRY SERIES

The National Poetry Series was established in 1978 to publish five collections of poetry annually through five participating publishers. The manuscripts are selected by five poets of national reputation. Publication is funded by the Copernicus Society of America, James A. Michener, Edward J. Piszek, the Lannan Foundation, and the Andrew W. Mellon Foundation.

1992 Competition

Shorter Poems, by Gerald Burns.
Selected by Robert Creeley. Dalkey Archive Press.

My Alexandria, by Mark Doty.
Selected by Philip Levine. University of Illinois Press.

Lost Body, by Terry Ehret.
Selected by Carolyn Kizer. Copper Canyon Press.

Debt, by Mark Levine.
Selected by Jorie Graham. William Morrow & Co.

What We Don't Know About Each Other, by Lawrence Raab.
Selected by Stephen Dunn. Viking Penguin.

THE PENGUIN POETS

WHAT WE DON'T KNOW ABOUT EACH OTHER

Lawrence Raab was born in Pittsfield, Massachusetts, in 1946.
He received a B.A. from Middlebury College and an M.A. from
Syracuse University. He has received the Bess Hokin Award
from *Poetry*, a Junior Fellowship from the University of
Michigan Society of Fellows, and grants from the National
Endowment for the Arts and the Massachusetts Council on the
Arts. His poems have appeared in numerous magazines including
Poetry, *The New Yorker*, *The Paris Review*, *The Kenyon Review*,
The Nation, and *Salmagundi*. He is the author of three previous
collections of poems, *Mysteries of the Horizon* (Doubleday, 1972).
The Collector of Cold Weather (The Ecco Press, 1976), and *Other
Children* (Carnegie-Mellon University Press, 1987). His poems
have been included in several anthologies including *The Best
American Poetry 1992* and the Third Edition of *The Norton
Anthology of Poetry*. He is Professor of English at Williams
College in Williamstown, Massachusetts, where he has taught
since 1976. *What We Don't Know About Each Other* was chosen as a
National Book Award finalist.

LAWRENCE RAAB

WHAT WE DON'T KNOW ABOUT EACH OTHER

PENGUIN BOOKS

PENGUIN BOOKS
Published by the Penguin Group
Penguin Books USA Inc., 375 Hudson Street,
New York, New York 10014, U.S.A.
Penguin Books Ltd, 27 Wrights Lane, London W8 5TZ, England
Penguin Books Australia Ltd, Ringwood, Victoria, Australia
Penguin Books Canada Ltd, 10 Alcorn Avenue,
Toronto, Ontario, Canada M4V 3B2
Penguin Books (N.Z.) Ltd, 182–190 Wairau Road,
Auckland 10, New Zealand

Penguin Books Ltd, Registered Offices:
Harmondsworth, Middlesex, England

First published in Penguin Books 1993

10   9   8   7   6   5   4   3   2

Page xi constitutes an extension of this copyright page.

LIBRARY OF CONGRESS CATALOGING-IN-PUBLICATION DATA
Raab, Lawrence, 1946–
    What we don't know about each other / Lawrence Raab.
      p.   cm.
    ISBN 0 14 058.701 2
    I. Title.
    PS3568.A2W47   1993
    811'.54—dc20   93–2664

Printed in the United States of America
Set in Bembo
Designed by Lucy Albanese

FOR JUDY

ACKNOWLEDGMENTS

The Denver Quarterly: "The Sudden Appearance of
  a Monster at a Window"
The Journal: "The Bad Muse," "Bad Dog"
The Kenyon Review: "The Other World," "Happiness,"
  "The Shakespeare Lesson," "Lies"
The Missouri Review: "Angels"
The Nation: "The Garden"
The New England Review: "Dead Elms"
The New Yorker: "What I Forgot to Mention,"
  "What We Don't Know About Each Other,"
  "The House on the Borderland"
The Paris Review: "Since You Asked," "Old Times"
Passages North: "The Thing That Happened,"
  "The Weeping Willows at Home"
Poetry: "At Evening," "Minor Painter, Paris, 1954,"
  "A Crow," "Stories in Which the Past Is Made,"
  "What He Thought About the Party," "Marriage,"
  "The Secret Life"
Salmagundi: "Beauty," "Learning How to Write"
Shenandoah: "Magic Problems"
Southwest Review: "The Last Castle in England,"
  "What the Dead Know"
Virginia Quarterly Review: "Ghost Stories,"
  "Something Sensible About Desire," "Daily Life,"
  "The Uses of Nostalgia"

"The Sudden Appearance of a Monster at a Window" also appeared in *The Best American Poetry 1992*.

"Magic Problems" also appeared in *The Best American Poetry 1993*.

I would like to thank the Corporation of Yaddo and Williams College for their generous support.

CONTENTS

WHAT WE DON'T KNOW ABOUT EACH OTHER

WHAT WE DON'T KNOW ABOUT EACH OTHER

In the next room my youngest daughter
is practicing the piano. I don't know why
that halting scale has made me think
of writing to you, after so many years.
Isn't it always the weather one begins with?
Here there is still a little color left,
the bronze of the oaks, pale yellows
of the lesser trees. Three or four
warm days in October are what we believe
we're entitled to, but that turned into a week,
then another, until we felt blessed
and disconcerted. Today the children and I
discovered a small patch of ice
and we were excited to have found it,
bright and brittle, full of shapes.
I walked them out to the bus stop;
they ran on ahead, and back to me.
It was one of those mornings
when you feel the season change, and you think
tomorrow you'll have it again
even more keenly. I remembered others.
I thought of how, looking a long way back,
I expect always to uncover some personal design
in everything. And so it's there,
by chance, by mistake, by necessity.
All the moments that might have gone differently
become the scraps of stories I run through
while falling asleep, so similar
in their melancholy heroism, their few
predictable cruelties. For all I know
you may have given up thinking about me.
For all you know I may have died,
a sudden tragic illness, or perhaps
the time my car spun out of control on the ice.
What they say is true—everything slows down

to a long arc, and though you do the right
or the wrong thing with the wheel, whichever
way you're supposed to turn it, the car
goes on as if you'd been abandoned, or released.
So there was an odd disappointment
plowing into that snowbank, the snap
of the seatbelts telling me I was safe,
then the stupid difficulties of getting out.
Later I could afford to be afraid,
when it didn't matter. Then I just stood there,
looking around me at the fields
and a small grove of pine trees
where snow was sliding off the heavy branches
very quietly and very slowly. That whole scene
was so sharp and certain, so *new*, I thought
I should feel as if I'd been given a second life.
Then would I decide to write to you,
hoping to explain how often I'd wished this
or that day had gone differently, and you or I
had spoken as we never did?
Now she's moved on to a song—"Waltz,"
or "The Three Boatmen." You'd laugh
to think it was a song at all,
but inside those stiff, hesitant repetitions
I can hear the melody she's after. What we know
or don't know about each other—
it doesn't matter, except that I've
moved beyond these careful inventions.
And that young woman you saw this morning
hurrying out of the library, fastening her coat,
looked like me only for a moment. There was
ice on the pathway, the sweet possibility
of snow in the air, all of the necessary
appearances of change—and yet the life
you've taken up to make this letter
could not be my life, just as this voice
was never mine, nor even yours.

1

A CROW

Here is the strict, abstract
light of winter. From a bare branch
a crow takes flight, rising
heavily, overcoming
the impossible. Snow
sifts from its branch.
A white shawl.
Thousands of separate flakes.
The bird has moved to another tree,
cawing harshly, though I can
barely hear it, with the windows
locked in place against
the cold. So the mind
remains at a distance
from its concerns,
its uncertain desires—
nothing to think of, or to say,
nothing truly seen until later.

WHAT THE DEAD KNOW

For the living know that they shall die: but the dead
know not any thing, neither have they any more a
reward; for the memory of them is forgotten. Also
their love, and their hatred, and their envy, is now
perished.

—*Ecclesiastes, 9*

When my mother died she took others with her,
all those whom she remembered,
whose stories no one else had learned.
Some of them continue to stare at me
from the cracked photograph, and I know
I've betrayed them, who can think of only
one or two names. Three generations
in their best clothes looking sternly
at the photographer—surely
they'd have considered it a small reward
to go on, as we say, in memory,
and must have consoled themselves
with the more joyful passages
of the other testament, promises
of a place where they would meet again
all whom they had cared for, would recall
everything age had blurred and stolen away—
be healed, restored, the human pain washed off
like dust from the road. This world
is still a difficult home, which they accepted,
although their children's children now
may look no farther. And then the dead
know nothing, and are nowhere.
Whatever spirit wanders down these long hallways
at night when the wind lifts the curtains
high into the old bare rooms—soon

she will find no boards to set her foot on,
no windows to gaze into, no glass
anywhere that will return her face,
her envy of this world,
like ours of the next.

BEAUTY

to M. D.

Is it wrong to imagine that in our lives
this or that should not have happened?
We choose to think spirit is a triumph
over all kinds of adversity.
Then we praise the spirit, praise
the hard times that made it what it has become.
This may even be true. As it is possible
to imagine the rich in their mansions
longing for the honesty of the poor.
The man with everything
looks down the barrel of his gun,
which is loneliness. And the homeless
wrapped in newspapers on the heating grates
know exactly what money will buy.
Let happiness follow if it can.
Let others argue for the purity of the cold.
Beauty cannot be as common
as all these glossy figures. And yet
there are those who are that lovely,
and who does not desire to be seen by them,
smiled at, seized and overwhelmed?
Some of us were lucky, some were not. Justice
is different, a place
where cruelties can be seen through
and then revised. So the solitary man
puts down his gun, decides he will live.
The night, after all, is calm. A moon is rising.
The great lawn sweeps off toward the sea.
Bring those perfect forms down here to us
and let their edges all be smoothed another way
so we will know that face even in the dark.
Everything that happened
happened. But you should never
have been told you weren't beautiful.

LIES

In Sunday School we talked about lies
and if it was ever right to tell them.
What if you could save someone's life?
What would God care about then?
We were in favor of saving someone's life,
though more anxious to defend the lie
and win the argument.
The world outside was quiet.
When the President said we weren't involved
our parents saw no reason for concern.

Later there was the story of the house
and the fire and what you would save
if you could save only one thing—
the cat, the Rembrandt, sometimes
even a grandmother was involved. Then
the lifeboat: how six could live
if one would consent to die.
It was suicide or murder,
all the extremities without detail.

Soon we were told salvation
lay in saying what we really felt.
So men and women explained everything
they'd always disliked about each other,
and some looked farther back
to discover what should be troubling them.
It was necessary to learn how to cry
in front of others who didn't know your name.

Who could excuse anyone else?
We returned to secrets, business trips
to Akron and Detroit when there was no business,
diaries and locked drawers, private correspondence.
And few of us worried about God, having decided

we could forgive ourselves
when the time came for it.

Houses burned in the cities
and nothing was rescued.
Because there was too much to understand
we were told to trust
the experts. We were told
forty percent might survive.
The stories we read had no endings,
just the details of this life
or that one, men and women
who believed that lies sounded like the truth,
or as much like the truth
as anything they could remember.

LEARNING HOW TO WRITE

The whole thing looks like things that
would show up anywhere around here.

—Derek, Grade 5

It's cold outside, or it's dark.
It's raining, or it could be.
Why not begin with that?
In the bright sun the trees
are perfectly still,
which only a moment ago thrashed about
in the storm. Similar things
happen elsewhere. The sky
is a sheet of blue paper, which may lead
to an ocean, or sorrow.
There are streets and pathways,
and people stroll along them.
Or just yourself. Or your father.
It's years ago and he's happy
having learned he's becoming your father.
You see how easy it is. Things
show up, and you gather them together,
things that look like anything
that might be around here.
Now you're walking home from school,
the day the dog chased you
into the street and the car
almost hit you. And it's possible now
to see the funeral, your small coffin
(because, in fact, you were hit)
the way they lower it so carefully,
the way they don't start
shoveling the dirt on top of you
until the family has left.
It's cold outside, and it's dark.

But you can follow them home, you can be
a ghost in the corner of your own room,
and at night you can listen, and find out
how much they really miss you.
And after you've heard enough
you might decide to be back
in your body, waiting on the corner
by the curb, so when the dog comes out
you turn on him with the stick
you've given yourself, except
this time maybe it should be raining,
not hard but steadily, and all the cars
are moving very slowly and very carefully
since at any moment and for no reason
someone might run out there.

MINOR PAINTER, PARIS, 1954

The day after Matisse died,
he was walking through a park
and for the first time he saw
what the human body looks like.
He saw the space that pressed in
upon the head, the gaze that turned
toward him, and passed.

That night he told Alberto, who nodded,
said it was true, and therefore
impossible, and as he spoke he scratched
a pencil across the paper in front of him
until there was a head, a man walking,
and the space crowding in around this man.
You see it is so simple, Alberto said,
but it cannot be done.

Others arrived, drank, told stories.
He knew a joke that amused them all.
Later they talked about Matisse.

When he left a man hurried by
in the rainy street. He looked
but there was nothing to see—
nothing but a man turning a corner,
a woman leaning in a doorway
lighting a cigarette,
the brief glow of her match, smoke
rising among the dark buildings.
There was only a street.

He felt the weight of his own body,
and then a specific sadness
out of which—he knew quite clearly—
nothing could be made.

THE SHAKESPEARE LESSON

for John Reichert

None of the students liked Cleopatra.
   She was selfish, they said, and Antony
was a wimp—because he wouldn't decide
   how he felt, because he ran away,
and couldn't even kill himself.

They were so impatient
   with the languors of Egypt, the perfume
and the barges, those fond little games
   he felt so close to.
Is there anyone you admire? he asked,

himself half in love with Cleopatra.
   Caesar, one student answered,
because Caesar knew what he wanted.
   The sun caught in the smudged-up
panes of glass; he fiddled with the lectern.

Could he tell them Caesar
   was the wrong answer?
Antony, after all, had betrayed the man
   his soldiers needed him to be.
And Cleopatra was foolish, unpredictable . . .

Could he ask them not to feel
   so certain about what they felt?
He said it was complicated.
   Why does it have to be complicated?
someone asked. Is that always good?

And shouldn't they have talked,
   figured out what they meant

to each other? Why does everybody
   always have to die?
Let's look at the last scene, he said,

and saw a stage crowded with bodies,
   saw her body displayed among the others.
How does it make you feel?
   he asked, although he did not know anymore
what he wanted them to say.

THE BAD MUSE

Calm down. No one's listening. Of course
you have the right to make mistakes.
Say anything you want, any dumb thing
that occurs to you. On the other hand,
it really does look bad, doesn't it?

And if anyone were foolish enough to print it
scorn and ridicule would be heaped upon you,
upon your family as well.
Think about them, if not yourself.
Someone in New Hampshire or California

is writing the important poem about history
at this very moment. Most of it
is done already. And this person
has had a life of great interest,
full of struggle and incident, whereas yours

is the same old life a thousand people
have had the good sense to keep to themselves.
Who wants to hear about what it was like
to turn forty, or the strange thing
your dog did last week? So relax.

Think of how good it will feel
to climb into bed and turn off the light.
And tomorrow is Sunday. You can read the papers,
go for a walk, cook outside. Friends will drop by.
Why not invite them all to stay for dinner?

And when the conversation gets really lively
and they're nodding in agreement
with everything you say, maybe someone
will ask you to tell that story—you know,
the one about the dog and the squirrel.

BAD DOG

"Just remember," my friend told me,
"you can't take it personally."
We were talking about the new dog
who ate things—a book one night, then
a pair of glasses—who clawed at the screens
when we were gone. How much remorse
would be sufficient? She lay down
on her back, legs up, eyes
averted. She gave herself over
to whatever cruelties we couldn't
manage to inflict, who were wondering
what it would mean, hours later, to brandish
the shredded piece of evidence and proclaim
the single, necessary word—
"No, no!" we insisted, and of course
she cast her eyes to the wall
and the way she trembled beneath us
looked like compliance, and then
almost like understanding, almost like
those bargains we make
every day when we talk to each other.

THE THING THAT HAPPENED

He loves someone else
and she loves someone else, but he isn't
the man she thought he was
which might be said for her, though he
could not have known
the thing that happened when she was young.
A friend betrays them, and lives to regret it.
Another pulls the strings
seventy-five stories up, and really is her father,
or his father, or both.
There's a gun in the safe, and he will have to use it.
There are papers that explain everything.
But you should have told me, someone says,
looking off beyond the terrace
where the sea is a bright field of green and blue.
I couldn't, someone else replies.
Now you know the reason.
Then they throw themselves at each other.
Father! they exclaim. Mother! Darling!

And then there are the ancient secrets,
dark, forbidden, sourceless.
The cemetery in the woods, the house
no one will walk past at night.
It's always been that way, the old man explains,
and I've lived here all my life.
But why, they ask, didn't you tell us?
Because you didn't need to know, he says.
Until tonight. And each is thinking, That's why
we got the house so cheaply,
why the neighbors seemed so distant,
why the thing that happened
had to, and will again. And when it's over,

with the sun rising, gray and dim, above the forest,
each feels different, somehow changed.
Father, he thinks. Sweetheart, she whispers.
Then they hear the birds
singing, the ordinary birds
that call out like this, every morning, to each other.

THE SUDDEN APPEARANCE OF
A MONSTER AT A WINDOW

Yes, his face really is so terrible
you cannot turn away. And only
that thin sheet of glass between you,
clouding with his breath.
Behind him: the dark scribbles of trees
in the orchard, where you walked alone
just an hour ago, after the storm had passed,
watching the water drip from the gnarled branches,
stepping carefully over the sodden fruit.
At any moment he could put his fist
right through that window. And on your side:
you could grab hold of this
letter opener, or even now try
very slowly to slide the revolver
out of the drawer of the desk in front of you.
But none of this will happen. And not because
you feel sorry for him, or detect
in his scarred face some helplessness
that shows in your own as compassion.
You will never know what he wanted,
what he might have done, since
this thing, of its own accord, turns away.
And because yours is a life in which
such a monster cannot figure for long,
you compose yourself, and return
to your letter about the storm, how it bent
the apple trees so low they dragged
on the ground, ruining the harvest.

WHAT HE THOUGHT ABOUT THE PARTY

My husband's chief complaint was that we'd included
too many people who believed in outer space.
He made no distinction between those who were intrigued
by the problems of the Hubble Space Telescope
and that much smaller group who personally knew
someone kidnapped by aliens. Outer space
was all the same to him, endlessly uninteresting.
I have to admit I was bored myself
by the Hubble Space Telescope. I kept thinking
of the Artist's Renderings I grew up with, how close
you were to the Martian canals, for example,
with figures in the foreground to add a sense
of perspective and a little drama. But I'm one
of those people who believe any movie
can be improved by including a giant insect.
I like it when the aliens walk among us
and no one's sure they're there, when they take somebody
up in the ship to examine him, but you never really
find out why. They leave so little evidence behind,
and what there is gets covered up so quickly.
Mostly I keep it to myself, these interests.
It's nothing I count on, and you can imagine what he says,
this and that about the world, the one he cares for.
We wash the dishes, make sure there aren't
any more glasses leaving rings on the piano.
If aliens have been around so long
you'd think we'd understand
what they want. Instead we don't even know
if how they're acting is smart or stupid.
When it's time to walk the dog I say I'll take her
because I enjoy going into the yard at night.
The sky's spread out above me, clear and chilly.
Ordinary planes are up there, lights flashing off and on,

and of course the stars, and all the uninhabitable
planets, and then the others, where right now maybe
plans are being made, where everything's almost ready.
No one can say it isn't possible, not for certain.
I like waiting just a moment for something to happen.

GHOST STORIES

Out of a patch of fog, or the branches
of a broken tree, or as a light
suddenly aglow on the ceiling—
they assemble themselves, and briefly appear.

This time it was a beautiful woman
gliding into his room.
She said nothing, but I was sure she was weeping.
She did not look at me—it was not for me
she had come. And then she was gone
as if back into that light which was
all that she was, or a dream, or half a dream.

What stayed with him was her sadness
and his desire, later, to have spoken,
to have comforted her, as a father with a child,
or as a lover, offering the same few words—

"What's wrong? Tell me. What can I say?"
—and meaning them, yet also seeing her now
as someone he would never know.
So it becomes a story of ordinary unhappiness.

She is crying, she does not want him
to say anything, or to touch her,
just as she will not permit him to leave,
since he must remain a witness, turning

only briefly to the window
where moonlight edges the black branches,
and the wind that is rising
cannot be mistaken for a sign
from any world but this world.

THE HOUSE ON THE BORDERLAND

You couldn't have foreseen
how people in a story, quietly
talking among themselves
about their lives, or the weather,
might float away from their concerns
into yours. There they are
on the grounds of a vast estate
at the edge of some northern sea.
Lavish celebration: the great house
burning with lights, the guests
gathered on the lawn, indifferent
to the cold, the dew
which is so heavy it stains
the hems of the women's dresses,
weighs them down. How late
can it be? The yellow lanterns
begin to flicker. A man arrives
with a message, and soon
everyone is following him
along the narrow untended paths
which at any moment threaten
to close entirely,
down to the rocky beach
where something's been discovered,
something all of them must see.
So many have assembled, speaking
softly, or in another language,
while men in long coats
dripping with salt water
pull at the corners
of a tarpaulin, dragging
it over what's lying there,
swept in, cast up,

and you can tell how difficult
this is, how intent they are
to complete their work.
Sweat runs down their foreheads.
Several fall from exhaustion.
More ropes are handed over, lashed
in place. But you find yourself
farther away, and unwilling
to press forward, uncertain you want
to see what the others see.
You think you've understood
the tone of their sentences—disbelief
or wonder, then resignation—
as if all of this had been predicted
or some day would be.

THE LAST CASTLE IN ENGLAND

Ruined hedgerows and forgotten tracks
mark the position of fields now gone over
to bluebells, banks of primroses.
Follow the path through the sycamores
to the old rope walk; at the north end
the remains of a shelter may be found.

From the top of the hill there was a good view
of a stone church and a field with cows.
In the gardens: a miniature cottage,
the children's playhouse, where once
a real bear had been kept.

Here bracken and furze have replaced the heather;
notice the elder bushes, the wind-pruned
thorn trees. If you are fortunate
a kestrel will be hovering overhead, occasionally
kingfishers, which may be spotted
as a streak of blue light.

The myth was they would live here forever.
Or when they got tired of it, weary
of all that raw granite and the steady wind
thrown off the moor, bored even with the adventure
of living in a castle, they could build
another house, and finer gardens, closer to the sea.
There was no reason not to, if one desired it.

Sometimes, the guidebooks explained, surviving
family members lived in private apartments
while beneath them had been gathered for display
the significant treasures—a writing desk
with pens and diaries, the pillared cigar box,

the small Rembrandt, and the actual linen,
we were told, the original plates and silver.

We walked slowly around the great table.
The forks and knives shone. A small bell
would have summoned them from another room.
Outside on the public lawns, ancient knotted trees
were propped up with bars of fresh lumber.

THE USES OF NOSTALGIA

1

Twenty years ago there was a life for each of us
to turn away from
or embrace. A song returns to remind me
of what I must have felt,
and when it's over, I play it back again.
Each time it's true.
Don't we look beautiful in the picture
no one ever took,
the clear sky unfurled above us, the wind
ruffling our hair,
everybody's real life just about to begin?

2

I know nostalgia
wants to make the present
feel bereft: a way of pretending,
neither the truth, nor invention.

Homesickness
as a disease; sentimental
yearning for the past.

First love. Second love. All that brilliance
the years have blurred, if not disproved.
Making the big play and winning the game.
Season after season, someone does it.

3

Above us the fan was slowly circling.
It was a room in which others
must have made love often, and sometimes
both of them felt good about it.
As we did just then, our bodies
allowing us the aftermath
that's sweeter than desire—
and a whole day to follow
in which every small gesture
had already been explained.

4

Sometimes I can hear
the teacher in me speaking so passionately
about the world inside a book I'm sure
no one will leave the room
unchanged. Until I notice

who isn't paying attention, disappointed
when it's the prettiest girl
fiddling with her notes, no reader
for the poem so exact
it could make her fall in love.

And I haven't forgotten nights
when desire was an instruction
my body refused to believe.

Then we had nothing that was right
to say to each other.

5

Then it's not the past
I yearn for, but the idea
of a time when everything important

has not yet happened:
love, fame, happiness—
unrealized, yet certain,

like the moment when we take our places
in a theater:
that slow falling of the lights,

that hush
as the unseen curtain rises.

2

THE OTHER WORLD

1

There is another one.
It's under this world, and inside it.
Look at what we're looking at
right now—that tree, that hill.
Who can see it for itself?

Even in your own house sometimes
people refuse to understand.
You hear it in the way they talk to you.
They don't want to understand.
They don't believe your happiness.

So I used to think I shouldn't
say what I knew.
Who would listen, who would stop to talk
on such a pleasant evening?
But now you've stopped.

2

I know a story I can tell you.
One morning after a long and restless sleep
a man wakes up to find his room
has changed. Say a pot of flowers
has been removed. It might have been

something else but imagine flowers
for the sake of our conversation.
Yellow daisies in a white container.
A complete disappearance. No petals on the floor,
no stray green leaves. And then that night

the flowers are inside a room inside
his sleep. But the leaves
aren't fine and shiny now, the soil's gone dry,
and of course the man is sad,
of course he is. Because it's hard

to look at anything that's dying
and know you can't help, that this is just
some dream you can't wake yourself out of
to get a glass of water. But anyway.
By morning a table's missing, that wicker table

underneath the daisies. And this continues
until his room is entirely
altered, exchanged, that is, with the other
world, and his life, needless to say,
becomes an entirely different life.

3

I won't say that story
was my story. The truth
is different, it sounds
like some music underneath
all the other music that we hear.

Think of the future,
the bright shadows of things
that became themselves until
there was nothing else to see.

Think of a place you could be
walking into, knowing more and more
of what it can only become.

Like this place, anywhere
you might be waiting—

remembering the house you grew up in,
the green lawns you ran through,
one afternoon spent watching

rain from an upstairs window, listening
to it until those notes
as they fell turned into a single
clear sound.

4

Once I was walking through this same park.
I was much younger, and I didn't think
of my life as something I would
one day be trying to remember.

I thought of going home, perhaps
meeting someone on the way,
stopping for a while to talk.
I wasn't alone. My daughter held me

by the hand. She was still worried
about the other children, running past us
with their balls and kites, crying out
so loudly. We stopped over there

beneath that big oak. She was tired,
and we watched the kites swooping this way
and that, their long bright tails
swimming out in the wind, way up with the birds,

swooping and swinging out and flying away.
And then I was alone. All over the park
snow had fallen. And the tree
was creaking in the wind.

A few branches had come down
on the hard snow. Nobody's footsteps
led up to me, or led away. Yet I wasn't frightened.
I could walk across that snow

and not put a mark on it. And everything shone!
Ice on the branches, dragging them down,
so the weak ones broke, and shattered.
All around me they were shattering.

Nor was it just the ice but my heart
breaking, again and again, so I could
sweep the pieces up and see
each part of it,

so I could understand
what this world would allow, and what it wouldn't,
how far beneath the tree
the roots go clawing on and down.

I held the frozen pieces in my hand.
It became her hand again.
And we watched the kites a while longer.
One came unfastened, sailed away.

Others held to their lines,
so far up we could hardly see them,
until the children reeled them in,
when the wind was going, and went back home.

5

The tree knows, and the roots underground—
there is another world, and yet
I couldn't explain.
                    What's wrong?
they kept asking.
What's wrong? And sometimes
she would start crying, and then
they both would cry.

One by one they all went away from me.
You could tell, couldn't you?
I thought you understood.

When I'm alone
I remember looking down
at what I held in my hands.
                    A spark flares up
if I rub the pieces together,
it always does.
And I can touch her hand when I want to.

It's there now.

6

I had a dream. It was like
certain old movies you might remember.
I was following a road, a long driveway
leading to an old house. Elaborate
iron gates swung open by themselves
to let me through, and at that point the voice
of the narrator came on, so quiet
at first, then more and more insistent.

It spoke to me personally. It said
everyone was waiting for me.
And they were all right, they were
happy, even those who had been hurt,
those whom I had hurt.

Just then I saw the house. It was evening now.
Lights were coming on in the windows
behind which I could see figures passing.
But the voice said I had to go back.
I was not yet ready to join the others.

Can you understand how sorry
I felt for myself,
how much I wanted to go inside?

7

There are times when you have
only a word or two. Wind or snow.

Stillness, nighttime. They take you back.
Things my mother told me,
or my father, I thought I would never forget,
and now I've forgotten.
Forgot how I felt when I lost them.

Sadness, I suppose, until I discovered
sadness wasn't what I had to feel.

8

This afternoon, not long before
you stopped, I was walking through
the city, along the river
where they've planted flowers,
so many beautiful flowers. I went out
on the bridge just to look at them
from a distance, reflected in the water.

Then I came here, and because
it was such a fine day many people
were strolling across the lawn
with their children, many children
who were running up to the crest of the hill
and pointing. They were pointing
at something on the other side.

I thought I would ask them what it was
when they came back down, but everyone
went down a different way.
I suppose if we climbed up there now
we wouldn't know if what we saw
was what they saw. And it's gotten dark,
so we might not see anything at all.

3

ANGELS

Like not having your father anymore
to look up to, theirs is the same, sad necessity.
Having tumbled out of the immense vault
of the sky, they cannot turn back.

So they are clumsy, often silent
and confused. And some
have already forgotten their missions,
and some can no longer manage to feel forsaken.

Occasionally we find them
in bars and back-alleys, in public parks
where they appear so familiar
the fact of their wings escapes us.

If they speak it is without conviction,
and their few tricks
remind us of how easily
something can be made to disappear.

In this way they have learned
to live among us.
And if we think of our fathers
it is of the father who has grown quite old

and cannot listen anymore
to our problems
and wants only to talk about dying
but does not want to say the word.

HAPPINESS

I can remember only once feeling perfectly happy.
I was eighteen, a freshman at college.
It was October, and I was sitting on the lawn
behind my dormitory, leaning against a tree,
reading a book. It must have been Sunday.
Leaves covered the grass, though the oaks and maples
were still full of color, and the sky
was that bright and absolute blue
you see in photographs of peaceful country scenes.
The musty broken smell of autumn
floated on the air, that scent like a taste,
like the idea of change. People walked past
on their way to the library, others
slept in the sun, or read their books.
Certainly I had enough to worry about.
I'd made no friends, was not in love, didn't like
my classes. But I felt just then
at ease, and then, lazily, quite
gradually, completely happy—as if that afternoon
might continue indefinitely,
and lead seamlessly into everything
that was going to be possible for me,
which I would one day call my life. No matter
what I thought about it, this would happen,
and I did not have to think about it.
I imagined staying until dark, when someone
might come by to ask what was wrong.
.Yet there was nothing I needed to say,
since I had no reason for feeling what I felt,
since the landscape was like a beautiful picture
of where I was, and so, after a few hours,
I got up, without regret, and went back to my room.
This happened, although that doesn't matter

to you, who know about the truth of poems,
how I can't convince you by insisting on the real,
can't persuade you by claiming this I is me, or was.
And yet I am not trying to persuade you of anything.
There is no conclusion, no story to conclude.
And how poor, after all, how familiar
the details seem, without excitement, or surprise.
But I never felt that way again, nor do I expect
to feel that way again, so thoughtless
and solitary, so unaccountably happy.

MAGIC PROBLEMS

The magician saws a woman in half,
pulls a rabbit from his shiny hat.
How did he do it? But we know
our pleasure requires not knowing how.
An amateur in the audience
would be looking for specific moves,
judging the trick on skill alone.
No fun for him, just homework.

When I was young I discovered
a way to prove that God exists.
Just let your mind go back
as far as possible, past the apes
and the volcanoes, past the fish with feet,
back to whatever first made thing
—a big stone, fire, air—you can imagine.
Then you call whoever made that "God."

No one was much impressed by this,
though it was comforting to think of God
inventing the world, not above me
watching what I did.
The magician finds a burning torch
in an empty paper bag—
a good trick, but frightening
if we didn't know about illusions.

Lightning blasts the dead tree—
we're confident it's not a sign.
When the stars assemble into human shapes
we remember their names,
or looking up at them now I know
where I left the book that would remind me.

A stick snaps not far away in the dark,
and because I've seen rabbits

at the edge of this small woods
I call it a rabbit. Then a creaking—
like a screen door being opened
where there is no door—which must be
the weight of a branch
on another branch.
Or a man, trying to stand
very quietly, adjusting his position.

THE GARDEN

We were in the garden talking
about disbelief, how it was
a practical choice—you couldn't
just decide to believe

as no one could resolve
to fall in love.
We were talking about the past,
the hopes we had for it.

Then there were skies of all kinds,
nights into which we disappeared
leaving the rest for later.
Things were different then, we said,

as if that were not always the truth.
So the future was a grand park
where we strolled, observing
the monuments, the fine inscriptions.

Around us trees
were moving, and the flowers
were ghosts of themselves in the moonlight.
Inside, cool breezes unfolded

throughout the house, room after room,
like a sadness without explanation
although—we might have said it—
just as much like joy.

DEAD ELMS

Back in the woods they just stand there,
pounded by woodpeckers until the bark
sheds in brittle plates, and winter begins
to bring the bare branches down. But along
Main Street the tree surgeon's dented
green truck blocks the sidewalk, the crane
is up, shirtless men flex their chain saws.
Soon only the fresh stump remains, soon
a cone of sawdust, and a view of a building
no one wanted to see more clearly.
Later a spindly ash or maple appears, stapled
into place, waving from its three taut wires
little red and yellow banners. Sometimes
we imagine how it must have looked
fifty, maybe eighty years ago—
double rows of elms all the way
from Field Park to Cole Avenue—
and the deep languor of those summers,
the carelessness, kids on bicycles
gliding through the dense circles of shade,
fathers playing catch with sons.
And no one thought badly of the future.
Or they found other ways
to remind themselves
of what they would have to get used to
because it was going, or gone,
and there was nothing they could do about it.

SINCE YOU ASKED

for a friend who asked
to be in a poem

Since you asked, let's make it dinner
at your house—a celebration
for no reason, which is always
the best occasion. Are you worried
there won't be enough space, enough food?

But in a poem we can do anything we want.
Look how easy it is to add on rooms, to multiply
the wine and chickens. And while we're at it
let's take those trees that died last winter
and bring them back to life.

Things should look pulled together,
and we could use the shade—so even now
they shudder and unfold their bright new leaves.
And now the guests are arriving—everyone
you expected, then others as well:

friends who never became your friends,
the women you didn't marry, all their children.
And the dead—I didn't tell you
but they're always included in these gatherings—
hesitant and shy, they hang back at first

among the blossoming trees.
You have only to say their names,
ask them inside. Everyone will find a place
at your table. What more can I do?
The glasses are filled, the children are quiet.

My friend, it must be time for you to speak.

DAILY LIFE

We knew the rat in the crawlspace
was chewing on something essential.
But who'd go down to set the traps?
The house was ours—wasn't it my duty
to protect it? Woodchucks arrived,

nipped the heads off all the better flowers.
Deer browsed their way
through the evergreens. Beside the porch
ants assembled their castles, then moved
into the damp wall of the kitchen.

What fine idea of nature would let me feel
my house might as well be theirs?
By morning, moles had taken over the lawn.
I flattened their little tunnels
and felt satisfied. By afternoon
all of them had been built again.

"When those ants get a taste of this,"
the exterminator told us, "you just watch
what happens." He pumped the wall
full of poison. They wouldn't budge.
"Pinwheels," said the clerk at the hardware store.
"Moles hate those things. Try pinwheels."

The yard was a vast city, the house another.
I considered the advantages of resignation.
I thought of Thoreau in his cabin,
Wordsworth among his daffodils and ruins.
I thought of all the great poems
of sympathetic observation, how my poem
wouldn't be one of them,

though in the end it might still assume
a certain festive air, with many
bright wheels spinning in the breeze
as if some splendid party
had been happily concluded, the children
driven home, only the dutiful father
left out in the evening, smiling at his work.

THE MOON MAN

*Beginning with a stanza
by my daughter, age 10*

The moon was his
only companion,
shining down on him
if he needed company.

But sometimes he wanted
to be alone. Around him
he felt the movements
of small animals, knew

the larger ones were silent,
watching, good judges
of distance and speed.
The occasional cries

were persistent proof
only of hunger.
And sometimes, when he needed
company, the moon

gave it to him, rising
and setting—
edge of a nail,
curve of a sickle,

then the shadows of a face,
then diminishment.
His eyes were used
to the dark, the way it covered

the surfaces of things
and weighed them down—
branches, pathways, all the houses
with their lights still on.

SOMETHING SENSIBLE ABOUT DESIRE

If we agree that the truth is never
      only what we want to believe,
the urgent arguments of desire

still have the body's weight behind them,
      the weight of the bully who tells you
what to say and then makes sure you mean it.

So you are on your knees in the dirt
      and listening hard—*Say it!*
Say it again. Late at night

after another bottle of wine
      all sides of the matter
blur into significance, and the opposite

of what you meant is what you meant.
      "But that's what *I* was saying,"
everyone is saying,

and no one wants to go to bed.
      Too late now for the singular, the personal
example; but I know what I wanted to believe,

what you were saying—something sensible
      about desire, and how we hurt people,
and care about that, and do it anyway,

and some of us choose what we feel
      we can't afford to turn away from,
and therefore think about death,

which is the last argument:
      how it stands beyond
all that is merely true, how it only listens.

AT EVENING

for my mother

At first everything reminded us of you.
We couldn't help remembering, wanting
to talk about it together. We understood
this was the way grief works
to return us to ourselves—no discoveries
or revelations, just the old stories
full of incident and detail.

Then your death grew quieter,
a suspicion the world would always seem
vaguely wrong, as when turning a corner
we recognize someone who isn't there.
Or when a storm, pushed up for hours
against the mountains, swerves off
and only the ordinary afternoon remains.

Six years now: marking the time
season by season. So we say without thinking
of the first warm days of spring: "Like last year."
And when we decorate the tree: "Last Christmas . . ."
Left out, you move farther away,
no longer even the image of yourself
but an idea of absence, sad and abstract.

Around the house you never saw us living in
the ragged music of the crows does not
remind us of what you might have said.
It's summer, the heavy peonies shredding
out onto the grass. And at evening
the light is dense and delicate,
the mountains arranged in a purity of blue
tier after tier. So that a sense

of comfort begins to include me,
without acknowledgment. A last crow
clatters back into the pines.
One by one: fireflies, stars.
So many flickering emblems—and this stillness
in which remembering might not be an obligation.
You would know what I mean,
you would have known what I mean.

AFTER HER DEATH

for my father

You were never one for confidences
but at her funeral
you were ashamed because you thought
you should be crying
and you couldn't manage it.

You meant your grief,
and you wanted it visible.
We'd waited all night
in the hospital, not speaking
except to acknowledge

each new report of danger.
You said you'd cried later—
that was what you wanted to tell me—
but not now, in front of others.
And was that wrong?

How many times had I been asked
to console you? Perhaps
only then. I thought
of books she and I
had read together, the way fathers

and sons would talk of loss, of what
we cannot say about what we feel.
I said it was all right,
I said I felt it too. Perhaps
I never loved you more

than at that moment, but I also knew
how well I spoke, the pleasure
I took in explanation,
as I told you how love could not
so easily display itself.

OLD TIMES

for my wife's mother

For a long time she pretended
she could remember. There were little tricks
involved, schemes and inventions, or so we thought
looking back. There were ways to speak
that gave away almost nothing. She'd sit in place
like a doll, you said, like a china doll,
the beautiful clear skin of her face
set in no particular expression, as if that, too,
was something she had practiced,
stored up against the time she would have
only this part to play, and she wouldn't know it.
Other times, older times,
she could talk about. She could talk about you
as if you weren't beside her, but back
where there was still some shape to speak of.
When she wandered away, what was she looking for?
When she got out of bed at night, took the pictures
off the walls, and packed her things,
where was she going? Once
out shopping, she turned to you
as to any passerby on the street, and asked,
Would you mind very much if I came home with you?
Yes, mother, we'll go home now.
Then she knew who had taken her hand.
It must have felt like her wish had been granted.

STORIES IN WHICH THE PAST IS MADE

to my brother

There would have been a time when I hated you
so completely I'd have thought
nothing could overcome it.
And why was that?—since you shielded me
in the predictable violence of schoolyards,
and told me, once or twice, what I needed to know
before I discovered I'd have to know it.
I wasn't so unwilling
to follow you, whose clothes I grew into,
who had things first and when they were new,
then fought for all the permissions
I'd inherit—the cars and girls, and how late
was too late, or just late enough.
What went wrong between us?
Was there one truly bad occasion?—
or simply the years of ordinary silence,
being apart and coming back
for the celebrations and the deaths.
And then we felt it together:
that need to be friends, although friendship
wasn't what we could have,
only love, the love of restoration,
of repair. So much of the past remained,
and late at night with the house asleep
we found those stories
neither could have remembered alone,
stories in which the past is made,
and corrected, and made again.
And so, my brother—the one they loved
the best, being the first,
the one who died before I was born,
the one nobody knew—
at last we have spoken.

MARRIAGE

Years later they find themselves talking
about chances, moments when their lives
might have swerved off
for the smallest reason.
                              What if
I hadn't phoned, he says, that morning?
What if you'd been out,
as you were when I tried three times
the night before?
                         Then she tells him a secret.
She'd been there all evening, and she knew
he was the one calling, which was why
she hadn't answered.
                            Because she felt—
because she was certain—her life would change
if she picked up the phone, said hello,
said, I was just thinking
of you.
                I was afraid,
she tells him. And in the morning
I also knew it was you, but I just
answered the phone
                              the way anyone
answers a phone when it starts to ring,
not thinking you have a choice.

THE WEEPING WILLOWS AT HOME

We planted willows to make the backyard private.
They grew quickly, didn't mind the wet lawn
and the cold winters. As a boy
I imagined walking out and seeing
nobody's house but ours, imagined
being seen by no one. Soon
(though of course it was years) those sticks
had blossomed, were tall and lacy, swaying
and drooping down, killing the grass
in widening circles. Then two or three
crowded the house, started growing

into the roof, and my father had them taken out.
Now he says the others should go.
Why not just a few? I ask. Why not half?
Why not all of them, he replies. He's heard
they're weak trees that fall over easily.
And they're dirty, the wind
always pulls some branches down, so by April
the lawn is covered with debris,
and it's hard, he explains, to get anyone to come
and clean it up. What about the privacy? I ask.
But my father, who lives alone now, is thinking

of the task of hauling all those branches away,
that it can only get worse. And why
should he want to walk into his backyard
and pretend his neighbors' houses aren't there?
Last week I could see how careless we had been
to plant so many. They shaded out the maple
and the pine. But we needed green
all around us, and quickly, or that was what
I thought, what my mother and I

said we needed. Now my wife suggests
other trees that might replace the willows,

better trees, a variety of different kinds.
How many years will they take to grow?
But my father isn't listening.
Kids don't want to mow your lawn anymore, he says.
Then bring them down. Pull the stumps out
and let the neighbors' children slide past
in winter, as my sister and I did
before the willows went in, when the snow was hard
and fast, trying to make it
through five backyards—which was possible—
all the way to the bottom of the hill.

WHAT I FORGOT TO MENTION

for Judy

Things fall apart.
First a chair, then a table. We can see
the roof needs replacing,
the garden's overgrown. How easy
to think only of obligation,
to talk for hours and say
nothing surprising. One afternoon
a neighbor's tree is struck by lightning.
It falls. And the maples shelter tiny insects
chewing on their tender, folded buds.
Then it's summer. All the convenient emblems
—flowers, seasons, rivers—
shrink a little in the heat, that cruel
weather I wasn't going to speak of.
But you, dear, what did you remember today?
Oh, the mind leaps backwards
and we shrug it off: just one flower,
nameless, bent toward water.
We were walking by and you picked it
out of sympathy. Or you let it stay.
Long ago the petals fell off.
Why think of it? That stain of purple,
so small it could mean anything.

4

THE SECRET LIFE

1

In a garden at evening a man
walks slowly among the shadowy flowers,
feeling that familiar melancholy
as it surrounds him—still, full of promise.
Far off a woman might be singing.
Where had he heard that song before?
Someone in a story, following the pathways
of such a garden, might also
stop to listen, and perhaps
instead of sorrow he could feel
a sudden, incomprehensible happiness—
as though the whole world
were watching him, keeping quiet, and waiting
for him to understand it . . .
The sky is clear, lit up with stars,
and now the air seems cold enough
to imagine frost by morning, to imagine
how the flowers might be damaged.

2

When he knew the cancer had returned
he wanted things to be quiet.
He sat on his porch, looked out at his garden,
and finished his work. This is what
the newspaper tells us: Raymond Carver,
Writer and Poet of the Working Poor, Dies at 50.
At dinner before a reading six or seven years ago,
I remember how he turned the wine glass over,
turned it over before the waitress
could ask if he wanted anything to drink.
It was such a definite gesture.
It said: That's not in my life anymore.
Then he ordered a large Coke, lit another cigarette,
and we went on talking. Hours before
he died, the obituary reports, he spoke to his wife
about how much he admired the stories of Chekhov,
whose death he had described with such care
in the last story in his last book of stories.
Olga went back to Chekhov's bedside.
She sat on a footstool, holding his hand,
from time to time stroking his face.
"There were no human voices, no everyday sounds,"
she wrote. "There was only beauty, peace,
and the grandeur of death."

3

"What do you want for your birthday?"
I asked my father, making our drinks before dinner.
It was a question he always answered
with a shrug—another shirt would be fine,
another pair of socks.
"What I want you can't give me,"
he replied, and paused—
"To be ten years younger."
In a few weeks he'd be seventy-four.
Why ten? I wondered. Why not fifteen,
or forty? Was he looking
back to some moment in his life
I knew nothing about? He'd never tell me,
even if I asked. I gave him the drink.
"But nobody can do anything about that," he said,
as if, already, he'd said too much.

4

In Chekhov's "The Black Monk," the young student,
Kovrin, knows what he sees is an illusion—
that legendary monk who sweeps across the world
every thousand years, who chooses him
to counsel and support. Yet what a pleasure
to talk all night of beauty, and the idea
of genius, and the object of eternal life!
Then one morning his wife awakens, terrified
to find her husband laughing
and gesturing passionately into the air.
Yes, he admits. It appears I must be mad.
Don't be afraid, she cries. All this will pass . . .
But Kovrin turns against her
after he is cured. He becomes reasonable,
sad, and mediocre. Years later,
in a small hotel by the sea,
where the air is warm and tranquil,
Kovrin steps out onto the balcony
and hears a woman singing
something familiar—a melancholy ballad
about a young girl listening in a garden at night
to sounds so beautiful and strange
she knows they must form
a sacred harmony, not to be understood by others.
Suddenly Kovrin feels that joy he thought
he'd lost forever, and at this moment
the monk returns. There was no reason,
he says, for you to stop believing in me.
But Kovrin cannot answer, his mouth
has filled with blood, and his hands flutter
helplessly before him, as the black monk whispers
that he has always been a genius,
and that he is dying only because his body
can no longer contain that genius.

5

"I think," Chekhov wrote to his friend
Suvorin, "that it is not for writers
to solve such questions
as the existence of God, pessimism, etc.
The writer's function is only to describe
by whom, how, and under what circumstances
the questions of God and pessimism were discussed."
I don't think my father was remembering
a secret life. I think ten years ago
must have looked like a time
when he wasn't afraid of dying,
when he hadn't started to worry,
each day, about how painful it might be.
Although I'm sure of this,
I don't want to believe it.
But could I ask him to imagine anything less real
than pain? And what would that be?
Beauty? Peace? Any kind of grandeur?
When all he wanted
was not to feel what he was feeling.

6

At times I imagine a voice,
not yet any person's voice.
What can it describe? A clear sky
full of stars. Or sunlight
on the frost in a garden. And the sound
of water or of trees in the wind which make
a sound like water. Then the light
finds a room where two people
are talking. It enters as if it were
another person who had arrived
unexpectedly. What were they saying?—
these two who are quiet now, watching
the light, which has made their silence
singular, like nostalgia
or regret. One I recognize
as myself, while the other,
who is not yet my father,
leans forward, trying hard
to listen, or about to speak.

7

In the woods darkness arranges itself
into shapes. I walk outside, and the cut grass
makes a wide avenue among the pines,
which, in a dream, or a story,
might lead somewhere.
Someone could stand here for a long time,
letting the stillness of the evening
include him, feeling that affection
we feel for the world
when it lies at peace around us.
And when he understands he must be waiting
for something to happen
that cannot happen, he turns
and sees the lights of his own house
not far away, the familiar pattern
of the windows, which he will look up into
as he walks back, thinking
he could still be anyone
out there with the darkness around him,
until he reaches the door, until he walks inside.